ASTERIX
AND CLEOPATRA

TEXT BY GOSCINNY

DRAWINGS BY UDERZO

TRANSLATED BY ANTHEA BELL AND DEREK HOCKRIDGE

HODDER DARGAUD

LONDON SYDNEY AUCKLAND

ASTERIX IN OTHER COUNTRIES

Australia	Hodder Dargaud, Rydalmere Business Park, 10/16 South Street, Rydalmere, N.S.W. 2116, Australia
Austria	Delta Verlag, Postfach 1215, 7 Stuttgart 1, West Germany
Belgium	Dargaud Bénélux, 3 rue Kindermans, 1050 Brussels, Belgium
Brazil	Record Distribuidora, Rua Argentina 171, 20921 Rio de Janeiro, Brazil
Canada	Dargaud Canada, 307 Benjamin Hudon, St Laurent, Montreal H4N 1J1, Canada
Denmark	Serieforlaget A/S (Gutenberghus Group), Vognmagergade 11, 1148 Copenhagen K, Denmark
Esperanto	Delta Verlag, Postfach 1215, 7 Stuttgart 1, West Germany
Finland	Sanoma Corporation, P.O. Box 107, 00381 Helsinki 38, Finland
France	Dargaud Editeur, 12 Rue Blaise Pascal, 92201 Neuilly sur Seine, France *(titles up to and including Asterix in Belgium)* Les Editions Albert René, 26 Avenue Victor Hugo, 75116 Paris, France *(titles from Asterix and the Great Divide, onwards)*
Germany, West	Delta Verlag, Postfach 1215, 7 Stuttgart 1, West Germany
Holland	Dargaud Bénélux, 3 rue Kindermans, 1050 Brussels, Belgium *(Distribution)* Van Ditmar b.v., Oostelijke Handelskade 11, 1019 BL, Amsterdam, Holland
Hong Kong	Hodder Dargaud, c/o United Publishers Book Services, Stanhope House, 13th Floor, 734 King's Road, Hong Kong
Hungary	Nip Forum, Vojvode Misica 1-3, 2100 Novi Sad, Yugoslavia
India	*(Hindi)* Gowarsons Publishers Private Ltd, Gulab House, Mayapuri, New Delhi 110 064, India
Indonesia	Penerbit Sinar Harapan, J1. Dewi Sartika 136D, Jakarta Cawang, Indonesia
Israel	Dahlia Pelled Publishers, 5 Hamekoubalim St, Herzeliah 46447, Israel
Italy	Dargaud Italia, Via M. Buonarroti 38, 20145 Milan, Italy
Latin America	Grijalbo-Dargaud S.A., Deu y Mata 98-102, Barcelona 29, Spain
New Zealand	Hodder Dargaud, P.O. Box 3858, Auckland 1, New Zealand
Norway	A/S Hjemmet (Gutenburghus Group), Kristian den 4des gt 13, Oslo 1, Norway
Portugal	Meriberica, Avenida Alvares Cabral 84-1° Dto, 1296 Lisbon, Portugal
Roman Empire	*(Latin)* Delta Verlag, Postfach 1215, 7 Stuttgart 1, West Germany
Southern Africa	Hodder Dargaud, P.O. Box 548, Bergvlei, Sandton 2012, South Africa
Spain	Grijalbo-Dargaud S.A., Deu y Mata 98-102, Barcelona 29, Spain
Sweden	Hemmets Journal Forlag (Gutenberghus Group), Fack, 200 22 Malmö, Sweden
Switzerland	Interpress Dargaud S.A., En Budron B, 1052 Le Mont/Lausanne, Switzerland
Turkey	Kervan Kitabcilik, Basin Sanayii ve Ticaret AS, Tercuman Tesisleri, Topkapi-Istanbul, Turkey
USA	Dargaud Publishing International Ltd, 2 Lafayette Court, Greenwich, Conn. 06830, U.S.A.
Wales	*(Welsh)* Gwasg Y Dref Wen, 28 Church Road, Whitchurch, Cardiff, Wales
Yugoslavia	Nip Forum, Vojvode Misica 1-3, 2100 Novi Sad, Yugoslavia

Asterix and Cleopatra

ISBN 0 340 04239 7 (cased)
ISBN 0 340 17220 7 (limp)

Copyright © Dargaud Editeur 1965, Goscinny-Uderzo
English language text copyright © Brockhampton Press Ltd 1969
(now Hodder and Stoughton Children's Books)

First published in Great Britain 1969 (cased)
This impression 1988

First published in Great Britain 1973 (limp)
This impression 1988

Published by Hodder Dargaud Ltd,
Mill Road, Dunton Green, Sevenoaks, Kent TN13 2YJ

Printed in Belgium by Proost International Book Production

The year is 50 BC. Gaul is entirely occupied by the Romans. Well, not entirely… One small village of indomitable Gauls still holds out against the invaders. And life is not easy for the Roman legionaries who garrison the fortified camps of Totorum, Aquarium, Laudanum and Compendium…

a few of the Gauls

Asterix, the hero of these adventures. A shrewd, cunning little warrior; all perilous missions are immediately entrusted to him. Asterix gets his superhuman strength from the magic potion brewed by the druid Getafix...

Obelix, Asterix's inseparable friend. A menhir delivery-man by trade; addicted to wild boar. Obelix is always ready to drop everything and go off on a new adventure with Asterix — so long as there's wild boar to eat, and plenty of fighting.

Getafix, the venerable village druid. Gathers mistletoe and brews magic potions. His speciality is the potion which gives the drinker superhuman strength. But Getafix also has other recipes up his sleeve...

Cacofonix, the bard. Opinion is divided as to his musical gifts. Cacofonix thinks he's a genius. Everyone else thinks he's unspeakable. But so long as he doesn't speak, let alone sing, everybody likes him...

Finally, Vitalstatistix, the chief of the tribe. Majestic, brave and hot-tempered, the old warrior is respected by his men and feared by his enemies. Vitalstatistix himself has only one fear; he is afraid the sky may fall on his head tomorrow. But as he always says, 'Tomorrow never comes.'

ALEXANDRIA, CAPITAL OF EGYPT. THE PALACE OF THE FABULOUS QUEEN CLEOPATRA, OF WHOM IT WAS SAID THAT IF HER NOSE HAD BEEN SHORTER IT WOULD HAVE CHANGED THE WHOLE COURSE OF HISTORY...

THAT'S AN INFAMOUS SUGGESTION, O CAESAR!

YOU HAVE TO FACE FACTS, O QUEEN! YOURS IS A DECADENT NATION, ONLY FIT TO LIVE IN SEMI-SLAVERY UNDER THE ROMANS

MY PEOPLE BUILT THE PYRAMIDS! THE TOWER OF PHAROS! THE TEMPLES - THE OBELISKS!

THAT'S OLD HAT! ALL THEY CAN DO NOW IS WAIT FOR THE ANNUAL FLOODING OF THE NILE!

THAT WILL DO!

CRASH!

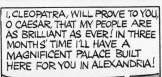

I, CLEOPATRA, WILL PROVE TO YOU, O CAESAR, THAT MY PEOPLE ARE AS BRILLIANT AS EVER! IN THREE MONTHS' TIME I'LL HAVE A MAGNIFICENT PALACE BUILT HERE FOR YOU IN ALEXANDRIA!

WELL, IF YOU CAN DO THAT, O QUEEN, I'LL ADMIT THAT THE EGYPTIANS ARE STILL A GREAT NATION...

...BUT I HAVE MY DOUBTS!

SHE'S A NICE GIRL, ONLY HER NOSE IS SO EASILY PUT OUT OF JOINT...

CRASH!

... PRETTY NOSE TOO!

SOON AFTERWARDS...

N.B. FOR THE CONVENIENCE OF OUR READERS, WE GIVE A DUBBED VERSION OF THE ORIGINAL DIALOGUE...

EDIFIS, I HAVE SUMMONED YOU BECAUSE YOU ARE THE BEST ARCHITECT IN ALEXANDRIA ...WHICH ISN'T SAYING MUCH

OH! *

* OWING TO THE FACT THAT DUBBING TECHNIQUES HAD NOT BEEN PERFECTED AT THIS PERIOD, THE MOVEMENT OF THE LIPS DOES NOT SYNCHRONIZE VERY WELL WITH THE WORDS

DON'T ANSWER BACK! YOUR BUILDINGS ARE FLIMSY! YOU CAN HEAR EVERY WORD THE NEIGHBOURS SAY! THE CEILINGS FALL IN!

IT'S THESE MODERN MATERIALS... ACTUALLY, WHAT I REALLY WANT TO DO IS BUILD PYRAMIDS AND...

SILENCE! YOU HAVE JUST THREE MONTHS TO MAKE GOOD. YOU ARE TO BUILD JULIUS CAESAR A MAGNIFICENT PALACE HERE IN ALEXANDRIA

DID YOU SAY **THREE MONTHS?**

IF YOU SUCCEED I WILL COVER YOU WITH GOLD! IF NOT, YOU'LL BE THROWN TO THE CROCODILES! YOU MAY GO!

THREE MONTHS! I'D NEED SUPERNATURAL POWERS TO DO THAT! I'D NEED SOMEONE WHO CAN WORK MAGIC...

GOT IT! I KNOW THE VERY MAN! HE CAN WORK MAGIC!

GLAC!

AND FAR AWAY, IN A LITTLE VILLAGE IN GAUL...

VI, VI, VI * AGAIN, IT'S LIKE MAGIC!

HA! HA! IT **IS** MAGIC!

THIS ROMAN GAME WILL NEVER CATCH ON...

* 3 SIXES

PEACE REIGNS IN THE VILLAGE OF THE INDOMITABLE GAULS, BUT IT IS SOON TO BE DISTURBED...

I'M GOING TO TRAIN THIS LITTLE DOG TO CARRY MENHIRS!

ARE YOU? MEANWHILE, WHY NOT LAY THE TABLE FOR US TO EAT THIS BIG BOAR?

...BY THE ARRIVAL OF A STRANGE STRANGER...

COULD YOU TELL ME WHERE TO FIND GETAFIX THE DRUID, PLEASE?

UP THAT TREE, PICKING MISTLETOE

GETAFIX?

WHAT A DELIGHTFUL SURPRISE!

?!

MY DEAR OLD GETAFIX, I HOPE I FIND YOU WELL?

AN ALEXANDRINE...

MEET MY FRIEND EDIFIS FROM ALEXANDRIA! HE'S AN ARCHITECT. I GOT TO KNOW HIM ON MY TRAVELS

GETAFIX, I'VE COME ALL THIS WAY BECAUSE I NEED YOUR HELP...

I HAVE TO BUILD CAESAR A PALACE WITHIN THREE MONTHS. IF I DON'T CLEOPATRA WILL THROW ME TO THE CROCODILES...

...AND UNLESS YOU USE YOUR MAGIC POWERS TO HELP ME I'LL NEVER DO IT! BOOHOO!

ARE CROCODILES NICE TO EAT?

SHUT UP, OBELIX!

DON'T WORRY, EDIFIS! IT SO HAPPENS I WANTED TO GO TO ALEXANDRIA TO LOOK A FEW THINGS UP IN THE LIBRARY THERE...

THIS IS MY CHANCE! I'LL GO BACK TO EGYPT WITH YOU

US TOO!

BY OSIRIS! WILL YOU REALLY?

WOOF! WOOF!

8

WE CAN CAST OFF NOW, SETHISBACKUP

HONESTLY, ASTERIX, I SWEAR I DON'T KNOW HOW HE GOT INTO MY BAG!

NO, NO, OF COURSE NOT! HURRY UP OR WE'LL MISS THE TIDE

AND WITH AN ICY WINTER WIND BEHIND THEM, OUR FRIENDS SET SAIL ON THEIR LONG VOYAGE TO EGYPT AND THE FABULOUS CLEOPATRA...

IN EGYPT WE SHALL HAVE TO CONTEND WITH LABOUR TROUBLES, THE TIME FACTOR, THE ROMANS, WHO WON'T WANT US TO WIN CLEOPATRA'S BET...

AND ABOVE ALL WITH ARTIFIS, A RIVAL ARCHITECT. HE'S ALWAYS GOT IT IN FOR ME. HE HAS A LOT OF TALENTS...

CLEVER, IS HE?

NO, RICH. HE HAS A LOT OF GOLD TALENTS — THAT'S THE MONEY WE USE IN EGYPT

AND THEN THERE'S ALWAYS THE DANGER OF PIRATES ON THE WAY

OH, WE'LL TAKE CARE OF THAT! RIGHT, OBELIX?

SURE ENOUGH, NOT FAR AWAY...

RIGHT, BOYS! WE'RE STEERING CLEAR OF ALL GAULS THIS TIME! AVOID ROMAN AND PHOENICIAN VESSELS TOO — THEY SOMETIMES USE THOSE. I'M PLAYING SAFE... I HAD TO LEAVE MY SON ERIX ON DEPOSIT TO BUY THIS SHIP!

NEXT INSTALMENT COMING UP, SIR! EGYPTIAN SHIP TO STARBOARD.

SPLENDID! WE'LL MAKE OUR FORTUNES! WE'LL DO IT YET! GET READY TO BOARD HER!

9

WHAT'S THE LOOKOUT SAYING?

HE SAYS THERE'S A PIRATE SHIP TO PORT

HONEST? YOU'RE NOT JOKING?

IT'S THEM, ASTERIX, IT'S THEM! YOOHOO! YOOHOO! COMING!

IT ISN'T TRUE! CAN'T BE TRUE! T'S THEM! GET OUT OF HERE, FAST! QUICK, SCUTTLE!

TOO LATE, CAP'N! THEY'RE SCUTTLING FASTER!

SCUTTLE THE SHIP, I MEAN! SAVES US A FEW KNOCKS, AND COMES TO THE SAME THING IN THE END

SOON AFTERWARDS

WELL, YOU SAID WE'D DO IT, AND HERE WE ARE, DONE! ALEA JACTA EST!

ONE MORE CLASSICAL REMARK FROM YOU AND I'LL MAKE YOU EAT YOUR WOODEN LEG!

OFFSIDE! FOUL! UNSPORTING!

AMAZING! THOSE PIRATES TOOK ONE LOOK AT YOU AND SANK THEIR OWN SHIP RATHER THAN FIGHT!

OH, WE'RE OLD FRIENDS... WE OFTEN GO SAILING TOGETHER

ONE NIGHT, AFTER A LONG, PEACEFUL VOYAGE...

WHAT'S THAT LIGHT ON THE HORIZON, EDIFIS?

IT'S THE TOWER OF PHAROS, ASTERIX. ITS LIGHT GUIDES SHIPS INTO THE HARBOUR...

WE'LL REACH ALEXANDRIA TOMORROW

A TOWER TO GUIDE SHIPS? THESE EGYPTIANS ARE CRAZY!

THIS, MY DEAR OBELIX, IS ONE OF THE SEVEN WONDERS OF THE WORLD!

NEXT MORNING...

AS SOON AS WE LAND I'LL TAKE YOU TO THE PALACE TO MEET THE QUEEN

AND IN HER PALACE THE LUXURY-LOVING CLEOPATRA IS SITTING DOWN TO HER FAVOURITE SNACK – PEARLS DISSOLVED IN VINEGAR

WHERE ARE THE PEARL TONGS, FOR OSIRIS'S SAKE?

HERE, TASTER! GET ON WITH YOUR JOB!

VERY WELL, O QUEEN!

THE GREEDY PIG! SHE'S TAKEN FOUR PEARLS AGAIN!

UGH! I DO HATE TOO MUCH PEARL IN MY VINEGAR!

EDIFIS THE ARCHITECT CRAVES THE HONOUR OF AN AUDIENCE!

SHOW HIM IN...

MEET MY FRIENDS FROM GAUL, O QUEEN – A POWERFUL MAGICIAN AND TWO BRAVE WARRIORS WHO HAVE COME TO HELP ME...

DOGMATIX!

GRRROARRR!

VERY WELL, BUT GET ON WITH IT! THERE ISN'T MUCH TIME LEFT, AND CAESAR KEEPS NEEDLING ME. IF YOU SUCCEED THERE'LL BE GOLD ALL ROUND. IF NOT– THE CROCODILES!

AND I WARN YOU, EDIFIS, YOUR RIVAL ARTIFIS IS NOT PLEASED THAT I CHOSE YOU AND NOT HIM TO BUILD CAESAR'S PALACE. HE'D LOVE TO SEE YOU END UP INSIDE A CROCODILE. YOU MAY GO

SHE LOOKS BAD TEMPERED, BUT SHE HAS A PRETTY NOSE...

VERY PRETTY!

14

DURING THE LENTIL* BREAK THE LABOURERS HAVE AN UNEXPECTED VISITOR...

* A VERY POPULAR ANCIENT EGYPTIAN DISH

... WHOSE REMARKS ARE EVIDENTLY OF ABSORBING INTEREST

TEEHEEHEE!

AND AT THE END OF THE LENTIL BREAK...

BOUHOUHOUHOU

... THE LABOURERS MAKE IT PERFECTLY CLEAR...

...THAT THEY ARE NOT GOING BACK TO WORK

MASTER! THE LABOURERS WON'T GO ON WITH THE JOB! I THINK SOMEONE'S BEEN STIRRING THEM UP AGAINST YOU!

ALL THESE WORRIES ARE POSITIVELY BLOOD-CURDLING! BY THE TIME THE CROCODILES GET ME I'LL BE QUITE UNEATABLE!

ALL THE BETTER! ARE YOU SO KEEN TO MAKE THEM A GOOD MEAL?

BUT THOSE ARE SACRED CROCODILES! YOU CAN'T JUST FEED THEM ANY OLD THING!

THESE EGYPTIANS ARE CRAZY!

IT WORKS LIKE MAGIC!

THAT'S RIGHT! TELL YOUR MEN TO QUEUE UP AND I'LL GIVE EVERYONE A DOSE OF MY MAGIC POTION

NO

OH, ALL RIGHT

NO!

HOWEVER DID HE MANAGE TO PENETRATE MY DISGUISE?

AND NOW THE WORK GOES HAPPILY FORWARD, TO AN ACCOMPANIMENT OF SINGING, JOKES AND PUNS, UNFORTUNATELY UNTRANSLATABLE...

GETTING ON NICELY!

SLURP! SLURP!

GRRRRRRRRR

?

GRRRRRRRRR

YELP! YELP! YELP!

13

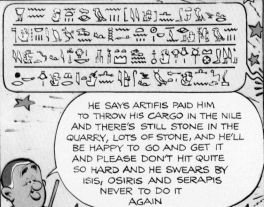

19

SOON AFTERWARDS..

WE SHALL BE JOINING THE NILE AND THEN FOLLOWING THE RIVER SOUTH

MEANWHILE, IN THE HOUSE OF THE INFAMOUS ARTIFIS..

I'VE LEARNT THAT THOSE MIRACLE-WORKING FOREIGNERS HAVE GONE OFF TO GET MORE STONE. KRUKHUT, THEY MUST NOT RETURN! THIS IS WHAT YOU HAVE TO DO...

THE FLEET GLIDES SLOWLY DOWN THE MAJESTIC AND SACRED RIVER NILE...

THIS IS SLOW!

VERY SLOW!

TOO SLOW!

ALL MOVE TO THE BANK! FASTEN THE BOATS FIRMLY TOGETHER WITH ROPES!

A BIT OF EXERCISE AT LAST!

BY TOUTATIS, THAT BOY NEVER CEASES TO SURPRISE ME, EVEN THOUGH I DO KNOW HE FELL INTO A CAULDRON FULL OF MAGIC POTION WHEN HE WAS A BABY!

AT NIGHTFALL THEY CAMP ON THE RIVER BANK...

LENTILS AGAIN! NOT A SINGLE SLICE OF BOAR! AND THEN THEY'LL WONDER WHY I'VE COME OVER WEAK!

TOMORROW WE'LL VISIT THE SPHINX AND THE PYRAMIDS. IT'S NOT FAR AWAY, AND THEY'RE WORTH SEEING!

BUT UNDER COVER OF DARKNESS A CUNNING SPY IS WATCHING AND WAITING

TEE HEE HEE!

16

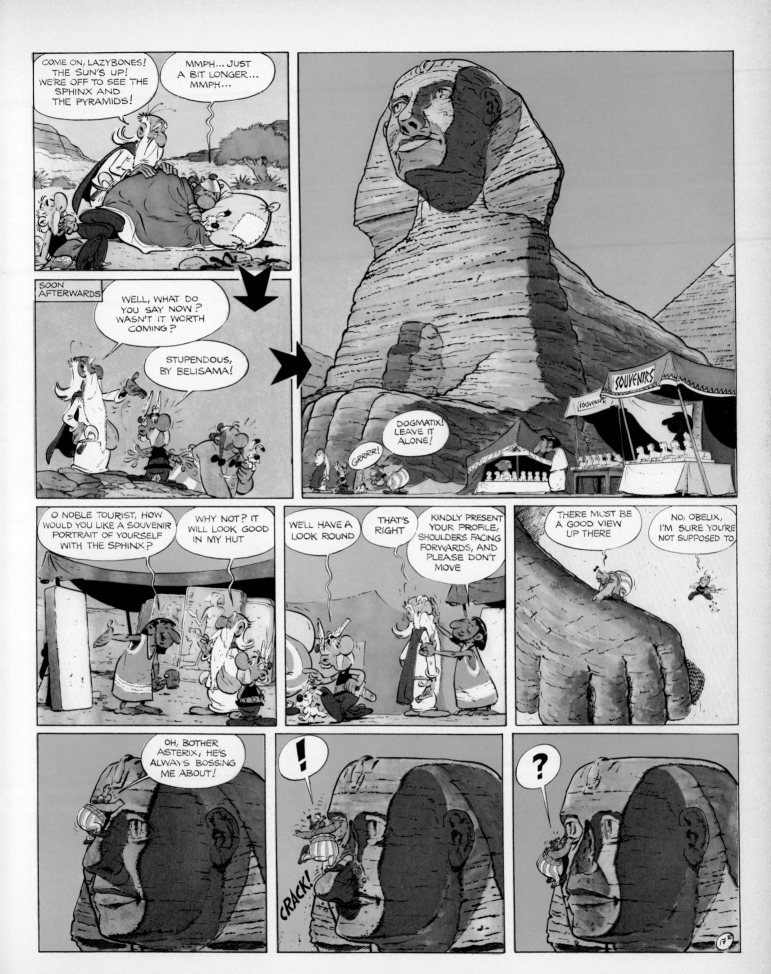

SO NOW YOU KNOW WHY THE SPHINX HAS NO NOSE. WHICH IS A PITY, FOR THE SPHINX'S NOSE, LOST TO THIS DAY, WAS A VERY FINE SPECIMEN OF A NOSE, IF NOT SO BEAUTIFUL AS CLEOPATRA'S, WHICH, AS WE BELIEVE WE MENTIONED BEFORE, WAS A VERY PRETTY NOSE INDEED

THESE PYRAMIDS BUILT BY THE EGYPTIANS AS TOMBS FOR THEIR PHAROAHS CONSTITUTE ONE OF THE WONDERS OF THE WORLD!

MAGNIFICENT!

HUMPH! GIVE ME A MENHIR ANY DAY!

FROM THE SUMMIT OF THESE PYRAMIDS, OBELIX, TWENTY CENTURIES LOOK DOWN UPON US!

WOULD YOU CARE TO SEE ROUND INSIDE THE PYRAMIDS?

OH, I THOUGHT IT WAS IMPOSSIBLE TO GET INTO THE TOMBS...

THESE EGYPTIANS ARE CRAZY!

THIEVES HAVE ALREADY BROKEN IN... THOUGH VERY FEW GOT OUT AGAIN...

BUT OF COURSE SUCH NOBLE VISITORS CAN TRUST ME!

WELL THEN, WE'LL BE HAPPY TO ACCEPT...

THAT'S NO PLACE FOR LITTLE DOGS... YOU WAIT HERE FOR US! IF YOU'RE GOOD YOU'LL GET A NICE BONE!

INSIDE THE PYRAMID

DON'T LOSE SIGHT OF ME. YOU'D NEVER GET OUT OF THIS LABYRINTH ALIVE

COME ALONG IN... THIS ROOM BOASTS SOME MAGNIFICENT HIEROGLYPHICS...

SLAM!

?!

YOU WILL NEVER GET OUT OF HERE ALIVE, FOREIGN DEVILS! THIS TOMB WILL BE YOURS!

23

INSIDE THE PYRAMID...

MY POWERS ARE NOT STRONG ENOUGH TO GET US OUT OF HERE... I AM VERY MUCH AFRAID THIS MAY BE THE END OF OUR ADVENTURES, BY BELENOS!

I'M ONLY SORRY FOR EDIFIS... WITHOUT OUR HELP HE'LL END UP INSIDE A CROCODILE

WELL, I'M SORRY FOR MY POOR LITTLE DOGMATIX... AREN'T I DOGMATIX?

DOGMATIX?!

YES, DOGMATIX! WHAT ABOUT IT? YOU'RE NOT GOING TO BE CROSS WITH ME FOR BRINGING HIM? ANYWAY, I DIDN'T BRING HIM, HE CAME ALL BY HIMSELF!

EXACTLY! HE'S FOUND US THANKS TO HIS NOSE... IN WHICH CASE HE CAN FIND HIS WAY BACK AGAIN AND SHOW US THE WAY OUT!

BY BELENOS, YOU'RE RIGHT!

DOGMATIX, IF YOU HELP US OUT OF HERE YOU'LL GET A VERY BIG BONE OUTSIDE!

YOU'LL GET TWO BIG BONES!

HEAPS OF BIG BONES!

OBELIX, I APOLOGIZE! YOU WERE QUITE RIGHT TO BRING YOUR DOGGIE!

SOMETIMES I FEEL HE UNDERSTANDS EVERYTHING I SAY!

21 XI

① THE FOREIGNERS HAVE DISAPPEARED. THERE'S NO NEED FOR YOU TO GO ON WITH YOUR JOURNEY
② I GOT IT FIRST TIME

IT'S MAGIC! YOU'RE WIZARDS! ONLY A SUPERMAN COULD EVER FIND HIS WAY OUT OF...

POF! POF! POF!

WHAM!

THE BOATS SET OFF AGAIN AND SAIL PEACEFULLY ON UP THE NILE...

SCRUNCH! SCRUNCH! SCRUNCH!

... STOPPING OFF TO SEE THE SIGHTS AT INTERESTING SPOTS SUCH AS LUXOR...

NO, NO, AND FOR THE THIRD TIME NO, OBELIX! THAT THING IN THE MIDDLE OF THE VILLAGE? IT WOULD JUST LOOK SILLY

WE SHALL NEVER BE IN CONCORD OVER THIS!

MEANWHILE, BACK AT ALEXANDRIA...

O ARTIFIS, MY MASTER... THEY'RE WIZARDS! THEY HAVE SUPERHUMAN POWERS!

!?

THEY'VE MANAGED TO GET OUT OF THE LABYRINTH OF THE GREAT PYRAMID!

FANTASTIC! THEY'RE JUST FANTASTIC!

ALL THE MORE REASON TO FIND SOME WAY OF STOPPING THEM! EDIFIS MUST NOT BUILD THAT PALACE, KRUKHUT!

AFTER A VOYAGE OF MANY STADIA ✳

MY FRIENDS! BACK AT LAST!

AND WE'VE BROUGHT YOU ENOUGH STONE TO FINISH THE PALACE!

✳ STADIUM: ROMAN MEASURE OF ABOUT 184 METRES. AS THERE ARE 30·48 CENTIMETRES IN A FOOT, AND 12 FEET IN AN ALEXANDRINE, IT IS EASY TO WORK OUT THAT THERE ARE ABOUT 50½ ALEXANDRINES IN ONE STADIUM

THE LABOURERS, WELL DOSED WITH MAGIC POTION, WORK SWIFTLY

IF I WASN'T HERE TO CORRECT THESE PLANS...

I'VE JUST HEARD THAT CLEOPATRA'S COMING TO VISIT THE BUILDING SITE!

SURE ENOUGH...

OH, DON'T STOP! I'M JUST PAYING A QUIET VISIT, INCOGNITO. DO GO ON!

THERE'S NO DENYING IT, SHE DOES HAVE A PRETTY NOSE!

A VERY PRETTY NOSE!

DID YOU SEE HER NOSE DOGMATIX?

MEANWHILE, IN ARTIFIS'S HOUSE...

AN IDEA! I NEED AN IDEA!

HELP ME! **AND FOR THE LAST TIME GO AND SHAVE YOUR HEAD!**

I CAN'T, MASTER. I MADE A VOW...

I'VE GOT IT! IT'S A PIECE OF CAKE!

SLAP!

28

WHAT DO WE DO NOW? SHALL WE BASH THEM?

DON'T DO ANYTHING! IF YOU RESIST CLEOPATRA YOU'LL BE HEADING FOR DISASTER!

SOON AFTERWARDS...

HA, GAULS! YOU TRIED TO POISON ME WITH THIS CAKE! YOU'LL PAY FOR THIS WITH YOUR LIVES!

CAKE? WHAT CAKE?

BRING IN MY TASTER!

SNAP!

HE TASTED A BIT OF THAT CAKE, AND NOW LOOK AT HIM!

IT'S ALL A MISTAKE, BY TOUTATIS! WE'RE INNOCENT!

* OOH, OOH, OOH!

I DON'T WANT TO HEAR ANOTHER WORD!

BUT...

IF THE QUEEN DOESN'T WANT TO HEAR ANOTHER WORD IT'S NO GOOD SAYING ANOTHER WORD, ASTERIX...FOR NOW!

TAKE THEM AWAY! AND GIVE THE SACRED CROCODILES THEIR APERITIF!

BUT WHY WOULDN'T YOU LET US EXPLAIN?

I HAVE AN IDEA...

BESIDES, YOU CAN'T ARGUE WITH CLEOPATRA ...SHE'S GOT A FOUL TEMPER, BUT SUCH A PRETTY NOSE!

29

GLUG, GLUG, GLUG

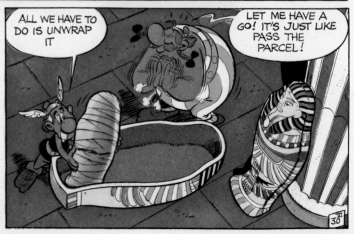

ARE YOU ALL RIGHT, EDIFIS?

NOT BAD... A LITTLE DIZZY!

POOR OLD EDIFIS, IT MUST BE ON ACCOUNT OF HIS SUFFERINGS!

I GIVE IN! I HOPED TO STOP YOU FINISHING THE PALACE. NO HARD FEELINGS?

NO HARD FEELINGS, AND TO PROVE IT WE'LL TAKE YOU TWO ALONG WITH US. WE'VE GOT A JOB FOR YOU

SOON AFTERWARDS, AT THE BUILDING SITE

THIS IS WHAT COMES OF ALL THOSE WICKED THINGS YOU MADE ME DO, BOSS!

SHUT UP AND PULL, WILL YOU!

THE BUILDING'S COMING ALONG NICELY, EDIFIS

THANKS TO YOU THREE, GETAFIX!

31A

MEANWHILE, IN CLEOPATRA'S PALACE...

AVE, CLEOPATRA. WELL, HOW'S THE PALACE GOING? TIME WILL SOON BE UP

AVE, CAESAR. OH IT'S GETTING ON NICELY, THANKS, JULIUS! WE'LL SOON BE ABLE TO HAVE A LITTLE PALACE WARMING

AVE, CAESAR!

AVE! LEGIONARY, GO AND FIND MINTJULEP MY EGYPTIAN SPY

AVE, CAESAR!

AVE, AVE, MINTJULEP. I LOOK LIKE LOSING FACE WITH CLEOPATRA...

I WAS TOLD THAT EDIFIS THE ARCHITECT WAS A NITWIT, BUT NOW IT SEEMS THE PALACE WILL BE READY IN TIME. GO TO THE BUILDING SITE AND SEE WHAT'S GOING ON, BY JUPITER!

31B

38

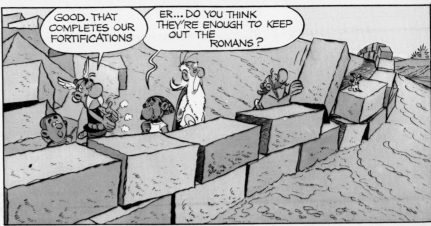

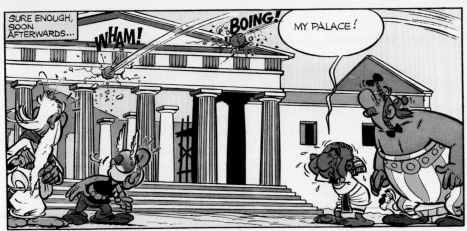

WATCH OUT! ONE OF THE BESIEGED MEN IS TRYING TO BREAK OUT!!

WHOOSH!

READY?

READY!

KERPLONK!

?

BOING!

HE WENT THE SAME WAY HE CAME...

JUST PASSING THROUGH...

SOON AFTERWARDS, IN CLEOPATRA'S PALACE

YOU WANTED TO SEE ME, O GAUL?

YES, O CLEOPATRA. MY LITTLE DOG HAS A MESSAGE FOR YOU

ISN'T HE SWEET! BRING A BONE FOR THIS LITTLE DOG!

THIS WILL NEVER DO! JULIUS CAESAR ISN'T PLAYING FAIR, BY ISIS! YOU MAY GO, GAUL! BY AMMON AND BY HELIOS, I'LL SEE TO THIS!

SCRUNCH! SCRUNCH! SCRUNCH!

KEEP STILL, DOGMATIX! WAIT TILL THE QUEEN'S NEW TASTER HAS TASTED YOUR BONE

GRRRRR

38

WATCH OUT! ONE OF THE BESIEGED MEN IS TRYING TO BREAK IN AGAIN!

WHOOSH!

HERE YOU ARE, OBELIX! DOGMATIX HAS JUST GOT BACK! HE DID HIS JOB PERFECTLY!

THERE YOU ARE! YOU SEE?

LET'S HOPE THE QUEEN ACTS QUICKLY. THE ROMAN MISSILES ARE DESTROYING THE PALACE!

SURE ENOUGH, IN THE CAMP OF THE BESIEGING ARMY...

THERE YOU ARE, CAESAR! EVEN IF WE DON'T CAPTURE THEM THE PALACE WILL BE DESTROYED JUST THE SAME!

EXCELLENT, OPERACHORUS, EXCELLENT!

AVE, CAESAR... ER... SOMEONE WANTS TO SPEAK TO YOU...

WHO IS IT?

ZING! BOOM!

TAPTAPTAP! TAPTAPTAP!

TANTANTARA!!!

?!?

ER... QUEEN... MY DEAR QUEEN...

THAT'S ENOUGH OF THAT! WHEN I HEARD WHAT WAS HAPPENING I HURRIED OUT OF THE PALACE AT ONCE! I DIDN'T EVEN STOP TO CHANGE!

OOPS!

WHEN YOU MAKE A BET YOU MUST PLAY FAIR AND I HAD A RIGHT TO CALL IN THE GAULS AND I'LL PROVE TO YOU THAT EGYPTIANS CAN BUILD BEAUTIFUL PALACES...

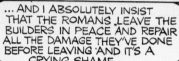

... AND I ABSOLUTELY INSIST THAT THE ROMANS LEAVE THE BUILDERS IN PEACE AND REPAIR ALL THE DAMAGE THEY'VE DONE BEFORE LEAVING AND IT'S A CRYING SHAME...

...AND...

ALL RIGHT! ALL RIGHT! DON'T GO ON! I'M SORRY AND I'LL DO WHAT YOU WANT...

ZING! BOOM! TANTANTARA!

PHEW!

WELL... ER... NOW WHAT DO WE DO ?

RAISE THE SIEGE AND REPAIR THE DAMAGE YOU'VE DONE, IDIOT!

AVE!

AFTER ALL, I WOULDN'T WANT CLEOPATRA TO TURN HER NOSE UP AT ME!

A VERY PRETTY NOSE, IN CASE WE DIDN'T MENTION IT BEFORE...

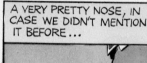

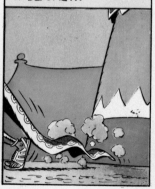

LOOK! THE ROMANS ARE RAISING THE SIEGE, BY BELENOS!

VICTORY, BY TOUTATIS!

AND ALL THANKS TO WHO ?

NEXT DAY...

NOT A BAD PALACE, IS IT?

HERE THEY ARE!

WHERE?

FOR YOU TO CUT THE RIBBON, O CAESAR!

O LOVELIEST OF QUEENS, YOURS IS THE HONOUR OF CUTTING THE RIBBON WHICH PROVES THAT I HAVE LOST MY BET, BY JUPITER! I YIELD WITH A GOOD GRACE BEFORE SO MUCH GRACE

THE CROWD ACCLAIM THEIR QUEEN, INVOKING THE SUN-GOD OF EGYPT...

RA! RA! RA! RA! RA

NOW WHO KNOWS BEST?

THAT'S A PRETTY KNOWS!

AT A BANQUET FOR 14,000 GUESTS (IT HAD BEEN PLANNED TO INVITE 13,000, BUT EGYPTIANS ARE SUPERSTITIOUS)...

YOU'VE SAVED MY LIFE AND TAUGHT ME MY JOB... MY GOLD IS YOURS!

NO, NO, IT WAS A PLEASURE. WHAT ARE YOU PLANNING NOW?

I'M FRIENDS WITH ARTIFIS AGAIN...

... TOGETHER WE'LL BUILD THE FINEST PYRAMIDS WITH THE SHARPEST POINTS IN EGYPT!

LATER, IN CLEOPATRA'S PALACE...

OUR WORK IS FINISHED. WE HAVE COME TO SAY GOODBYE, O QUEEN

THAT NOSE...

YOU HAVE PERFORMED MIRACLES, GAULS, AND YOU ARE ENTITLED TO ALL THE GRATITUDE OF THE QUEEN OF QUEENS: ME!

I AM MAKING YOU A PRESENT OF THESE PRECIOUS MANUSCRIPTS FROM THE LIBRARY OF ALEXANDRIA O DRUID...

YOUR NOSE... ER... YOUR MAJESTY IS TOO CHARMING, BY BELENOS...

WHAT A NOSE!

IT SEEMS VERY LITTLE FOR ALL THE HELP YOU HAVE GIVEN ME. I DON'T KNOW HOW TO THANK YOU...

ALWAYS AT YOUR SERVICE... AND IF YOU EVER NEED ANYTHING ELSE BUILT IN EGYPT—SAY A CANAL BETWEEN THE RED SEA AND THE MEDITERRANEAN...

...WELL, CALL ON SOMEONE FROM OUR COUNTRY, BY TOUTATIS!

SOON AFTERWARDS

NICE OF CLEOPATRA TO LEND US HER OWN BARGE TO TAKE US BACK TO GAUL...

AND THE CAPTAIN GIVES THE ORDER TO GO...

DING! DING!

DING! DING!

FULL SPEED AHEAD!

BOOM!

DO YOU THINK WE'LL MEET THOSE PIRATES AGAIN, ASTERIX?

I DON'T KNOW, OBELIX, BUT I GET THE FEELING THEY'RE NOT FAR AWAY!

SURE ENOUGH, DOWN IN THE HOLD...

I HAD TO TAKE THIS JOB TO PAY FOR MY LAST BOAT, BUT AS SOON AS I CAN PUT A DEPOSIT DOWN ON ANOTHER I'LL LOOK FOR THOSE CONFOUNDED GAULS!

43